Vickie grew up in Devon and moved to London a decade or so ago. She is a solicitor by day and a teller of stories the rest of the time. She now lives just outside London with her husband, Nick; son, Freddie; and cat, Kimi.

Rex
the
DRAGON

Vickie Broden-Keast

AUSTIN MACAULEY PUBLISHERS™

LONDON • CAMBRIDGE • NEW YORK • SHARJAH

Copyright © Vickie Broden-Keast (2019)

A CIP catalogue record for this title is available from the British Library.

ISBN 9781788783507 (Paperback)
ISBN 9781788783514 (Hardback)
ISBN 9781528955423 (ePub e-book)

www.austinmacauley.com

First Published (2019)
Austin Macauley Publishers Ltd
25 Canada Square
Canary Wharf
London
E14 5LQ

For Freddie, and all who tell him stories.

Thanks to my family, and to Nick, for your support
in this and everything.

This is a **dragon** called Rex.

His scales are as shiny as a marble, as colourful as lollipops, and he is the same size as you.

Rex lived in his cave all by himself. He did not have any brothers, or sisters, or anyone to talk to.

One morning, Rex decided to go and find some friends.

Rex went to a grassy field and met a bunny called Ben.
Ben was as white as milk, as gentle as spring, and he
could jump as high as sunflowers grow.

Rex asked Ben what he liked to do.

"I like to jump," said Ben.

Rex did not really like jumping, but he really wanted a friend, so he decided to change.

Rex changed into a **frog**.

He was as slimy as mud, as green as fresh peas and very good at jumping.

Rex and Ben jumped all morning, but Rex did not like being slimy, so he changed back into a **dragon**.

Rex went to a beautiful forest and met a blue **bird** called **Bella**.

Bella was as blue as the spring sky, her feathers as soft as flower petals, and she flew as gracefully as the clouds.

Rex asked **Bella** what she liked to do.

"I like to fly," said **Bella**.

Rex did not really like flying, but he really wanted a friend, so he decided to change.

Rex changed into a butterfly.

He was as bright as a rainbow, as small as a sugar cube and very good at flying.

Rex and Bella flew until lunchtime, but Rex didn't like being so small, so he changed back into a dragon.

Rex went to the deep blue sea and met a whale called Walter.

Walter was as smooth as rain, as big as a bus and he swam as well as the ocean danced.

Rex asked Walter what he liked to do.

"I like to swim," said Walter.

Rex was not very good at swimming, but he really wanted a friend, so he decided to change.

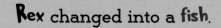

Rex changed into a **fish**.

He was as cold as stones, as wet as a waterfall and very good at swimming.

Rex and **Walter** swam all afternoon, but **Rex** did not like being so cold, so he changed back into a **dragon**.

Next, Rex went to the warm colourful jungle and met a monkey called Millie.

Millie was as agile as the breeze, as brown as chocolate and climbed as well as the vines swung.

Rex asked Millie what she liked to do.

"I like to climb," said Millie.

Rex did not really like climbing, but he really wanted
a friend, so he decided to change.

Rex changed into a tiger.

He was as fierce as fire, striped like jungle shadows
and very good at climbing.

Rex and Millie climbed until tea-time, but Rex did not
like being so fierce, so he changed back into a dragon.

Finally, Rex went to the freezing cold Arctic and met a polar bear called Peter.

Peter was as white as ice, as strong as wind and ran as quickly as the snow fell.

Rex asked Peter what he liked to do.

"I like to run in the snow," said Peter.

Rex did not really like running, but he really wanted a friend, so he decided to change.

Rex changed into an Arctic hare.

He was as clever as a fox, as quick as a wink, and very good at running.

Rex and Peter ran in the snow all evening, but Rex did not like the ice, so he changed back into a dragon.

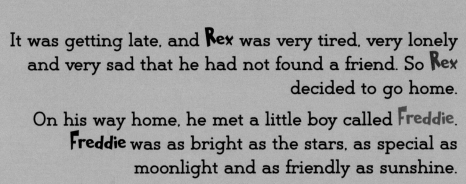

It was getting late, and **Rex** was very tired, very lonely and very sad that he had not found a friend. So **Rex** decided to go home.

On his way home, he met a little boy called **Freddie**. **Freddie** was as bright as the stars, as special as moonlight and as friendly as sunshine.

Rex asked **Freddie** what he liked to do.

"I like stories," said **Freddie**.

Rex was very good at telling stories. He knew a very good story about the day he went to find a friend.

He started at the beginning and finished at...

The End